TOAD'S TOOLS

ADRIAN M. HURTADO

Illustrated by Jayne Koontz

ISBN: 978-1-968970-22-2 (sc)
ISBN: 978-1-968970-23-9 (e)

Rev. date: 08/06/2025

The morning sun came shining through Toad's bedroom window. He leaped out of bed and quickly took down the tool belt that was hanging on the peg on his bedroom wall right next to the picture of his father. He strapped the belt around his waist.

Toad always wore his tool belt, except when he's sleeping of course.

Toad was very proud of his tools. They had belonged to his father many years before. They were left to Toad when his father passed away.

Toad's father was always using his tools to help others, and Toad wanted to follow in his footsteps. His father often said, "Nothing feels as good as helping others."

COOKIES
Krtter Krunchies
Baby Bugs
SLUGS
French Flies
5
4 12
1
7 6 5

Toad ate a healthy breakfast, then left his pad and headed down the path toward old Miss Bunny Rabbit's house. She always needed help with something.

"Good morning Miss Bunny," said Toad as he neared her house. Miss Bunny was in her garden tending to her carrot patch.

"Hello Toad," she replied. "I'm so glad to see you. The wind blew off one of my window shutters last night. It got quite chilly in my house."

9

"I can fix that," said Toad. He reached into his tool belt and took out a screwdriver. In no time at all, the shutter was up and in place.

"My kitchen faucet also dripped all night," said Miss Bunny. "The noise bothered me very much."

"I can fix that," said Toad. He took a wrench from his tool belt and quickly used it to stop the leaking faucet.

"You are wonderful," said Miss Bunny. "You're so much like your father."

Toad smiled and said, "Nothing feels as good as helping others."

After a piece of Miss Bunny's wonderful carrot cake, Toad headed down the path.

14

He came upon Furry Squirrel's tree house.
Furry was scurrying around and seemed
very upset.

"What's the matter?" asked Toad.

16

"There's a new hole in the bottom of my tree," said Furry. "Every time I carry nuts into my tree, they roll right out the hole in the bottom. I'll never be able to store enough food for my family before winter comes."

"I can fix that," said Toad.

He looked around and found a log about the same size as the hole. He took his saw from his tool belt and cut a piece off the end.

Then he took his hammer and pounded the piece into the hole as a plug. It was a very tight fit and would not come out.

"That's terrific," said Furry. "You're so much like your father."

Toad just smiled and said, "Nothing feels as good as helping others."

After a slice of Furry's special nut bread, Toad headed down the path.

The path circled around the forest and Toad was almost home when he heard a very excited chatter in a tree above. He looked up and saw Mr. Blue Jay with a very worried look on his face.

"What's the matter, Blue?" asked Toad.

"Mrs. Blue Jay will be ready to lay her eggs by tomorrow," said Blue, "and I haven't been able to find enough small twigs to build a good nest. Everything around here is too big."

"I can fix that," said Toad.

Toad removed his hatchet from his tool belt and began chopping some of the large twigs into smaller pieces. As he chopped, Blue gathered up the pieces and flew up into the tree.

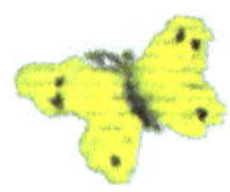

Toad kept chopping until he finally heard Blue shout down, "You can stop Toad. That's enough."

Toad sat down to rest. He was very tired after this last job.

Blue came down and sat next to him. "That was very nice of you to help," he said. "That is exactly what your father would have done. He would be very proud of you."

That made Toad feel so good he no longer remembered that he was tired. He smiled at Blue and said, "Nothing feels as good as helping others."

Mrs. Blue Jay flew down with a bowl of her famous bird's nest soup.

Toad ate it hungrily, thanked her, then got up and headed for home.

When Toad arrived home to his pad, he wasn't hungry for some reason and decided to skip dinner and get to bed early. As he looked up at the picture of his father hanging on the bedroom wall, a big smile came upon his face.

"You were right, dad. Nothing feels as good as helping others," said Toad, "and I'm proud to wear your tool belt and I always will."

...except when he's sleeping
of course.